ANIMA

ANNA CASAMENTO ARRIGO

PAGE PUBLISHING
Conneaut Lake, PA

First originally published by Page Publishing 2022

ISBN 978-1-6624-7172-8 (pbk)
ISBN 978-1-6624-7173-5 (digital)

Printed in the United States of America

DEDICATION

• •

For Ako

Acknowledgement

· ·

A tremendous thank you to Paul Simeone for the beautifully touching composition of my poems 'Closer,' 'Once Upon a Fairytale,' 'Through Papa's Eyes,' and 'The Perfect Distance.' (For your listening pleasure on YouTube).

FOREWORD

From the first time I read a collection of Mrs. Casamento Arrigo's poetry, I knew that she had a distinct and unique voice. Her poetry speaks to the mind and body of the reader, the heart, and the soul.

Poetry was never something I was interested in, but after reading her work, it touched something deep within me, the concept of looking inward while also looking outward and making that connection to the world at large and my place in it.

In her poems, Mrs. Arrigo shares with the reader the complexities of life with all of its cruelty, its impersonal nature, its joy at being alive, its rapture. She has the background for it. A stroke survivor—and someone who's thrived—she is well aware of the intransigence of life. That feeling comes through in her work all too clearly, but it is never down, always up, always pushing forward.

To have such an outlook is something special and dear, and I am privileged to have been given the opportunity to not only read her latest collection but also to write the foreword.

This is Ms. Arrigo's gift to the world: her essence, her soul, bared for all to see. May you take heart in what she has written and make your own connections as well.

Jess (J.S) Frankel, author of Catnip, Iris Incredible, Master Fantastic, and other young adult works

"CLOSER" (SONG VERSION)

ACArrigo and Paul Simeone

Will you be here
Holding me closer
Feeling my breath and sighs
Touching me now, filling my senses
Beneath the moonlit skies
And the sunset, and sunrise
We tasted the night
I fell into your eyes

Will you be here
Closer once more
Filling my every sense
Tender words catch in the air
I'm falling once again
And together, forever
I'm caught in your eyes
Beneath those moonlit skies
Closer to you

You'll be my each beginning
You will be my end
We'll weather each winter storm
Wanting, needing, yearning
Once more, then again
Just hold me now
Keep me warm

And together, forever
I'm caught in your eyes
Beneath those moonlit skies
Closer to you
Closer to you
Closer to you.

ONCE UPON A FAIRYTALE

(ACArrigo and Paul Simeone)

Once upon a fairytale
Asleep
I dared to dream
Of kingdoms beyond my reach
Circling over Meadows
Glens
A dwelling of sugar plums and gingerbread
Over oceans vast and deep
Peering down from atop
My unicorn with its rainbow wings
And wondered what undiscovered beauty laid
Underneath...
Dragons
Trolls
In that mystical place
Where the princess does sleep
Once upon a fairytale
Where a budding flower
Drinks up the morning dew
And nymphs pluck out a magical tune
Once upon a fairytale
Fleeting thoughts and...
Follies not...
This was-
IS
My dream after all...
Once Upon a Fairytale...
Once Upon a Fairytale-

THROUGH PAPA'S EYES

(ACA and Paul Simeone)

Papa drank himself to sleep
Before the moon would rise
And his little girl watched and wondered
What the world looked like through his eyes
Four Roses pouring out,
Again and again and again
With his little girl watching and wondering
If the pouring would ever end
See the world go dark as night
Through Papa's eyes

She could hear Papa talking,
Screaming in his sleep
As his little girl kept watch, wondering
'Bout the secrets he would keep
The ones hidden—tumbling down
With a sadness in his brain
As his little girl kept watch, wondering
While Papa drank away his pain
See the world go dark as night
Through Papa's eyes

Days passed and the years too quickly gone
As she watched Papa do just what he'd always done
And the dreams died hard
At the bottom of a glass through Papa's eyes

Such a sad and hopeless fight
While the world goes dark as night
Through Papa's eyes

THE PERFECT DISTANCE

I watch as they kneel down to pray
Thinking of the words I can no longer say
And in the perfect distance, I unseen
Wondering why did you have to be so mean
The perfect smile upon your face and I
Living in the shadow of a lie

(CHORUS)
Where does a devil sleep?
With all the secrets he will keep…
Why did you do that to me?
Why did you do that to me?

With mom waiting restless by the phone
And dad traveling oh so far from home
As the world stares and simply wonders why
Once believing the shadows and the lie
I watch the mourners under skies of gray
With angel wings my dad just made

(CHORUS)
Do hear my voice so small
Pleading out, "Ohh…"
Taking my breath, watching me fall
Pleading out, "Ohh…"

EROSIONS

I'd heard the thunderous clouds
just beyond the cyan horizon
where the playful wind
whispers
And I watched as Mercurian Angels
Held tightly that last collection of night stars-
humming in voices adagio e piene di gioa
I had spoken to the Asian Koel
Just before it joined that Seventh Choir of Angels
-and felt my soul float
upon the wind currents
somewhere above the Adriatic
and beyond the Khiluk—
it was just then…the now
that the Wind of Erosions
revealed…catching my glance
beckoned me-
Sing!

WHEN I DIE

When I die
I will not lament the golden road outstretched to its
Own will
I will not pine the hunger for unsatisfied passion.
I will not hold in judgment those seeking only my
survival when I yearned and sought to live instead.
I will not stand unwelcoming at the foot of the altar
All those before me who know not where I loved.
I will not yearn another second in the existence
of that translucent Solitude.
Alone I will not go forth-back and up Again.
I will not question the moment that will follow
All those that came before-
I will not hollow out my heart
Replace it with cotton clouds of doubt
This I will know
That I will know
And in the knowing will be my existence
Still.

A World In Chaos

Chaos in the world-

A fawn searching for its slaughtered mother.

Intelligent Women Bore Easily

• •

Ain't got no time to bare my soul

You're not listening in any case

Your boring dribble about the latest blah

Blah blah

Intelligent women bore easily

And idle chit chat

Like a junkyard car

Too long in the rain

Rusted

Seats torn up

Torn out

60s perhaps

And I'm guessing lovers

With only the blue moon as their witness

Fogged windows…

Then

Perhaps…

Intelligent women bore easily

—

And the cracked windshield

With non-existent wipers

As if-

Speak to me

To my heart

Dante

Shakespeare

Poe

Joyce

Hemingway

Dickens

Hansberry

Wilde

Williams

Frost

Langston

And Gwendolyn

Et all…

Heard the weather report

And, my, isn't it a sunny day…

Filler sounds

Intelligent women

Need no guised

Feigned

Forced

And the banal

Speak to my heart…

Music

Art

Literature

Poetry…most of all

Come now…

Do you really need to ask

'How are you today?'

And, all I really hear is Charlie Brown's teacher in the distance

Droning

Wahwahwahwahwah

RepeatRewindRepeat

Dom

Merlot

Beer

Tea

And lots and lots of coffee

Intelligent women

Bore.

Easily.

IN MY ROBE AND SLIPPERS

Open toed slippers

Catching Frost's leftover crystals

Between my toes

My body

My legs

A disconnect

Break dancing down the iced blacktop

Is that daily paper worth this breakdancing

Of memories frozen

Thawed

Only to re-freeze

Before they fade away

In the melting

Of tomorrow's sunlight.

Today's news…

The headline tomorrow

Can wait…

My Loves

I love the feel of snowflakes upon my tongue
Wishing I could catch them all
Before
In harmony blanket the earth
Soothing
Comforting
In contentment
Ease away weariness
Too long helplessly watching
Chaos-discord-and some
Righteous indignation
Respite…
While slightly below
Awaits the resurgence…rebirth of crocuses
Lavender
Daffodils
All…but for that winter's thaw
And April's quenching
Once again…life
I love the sound of children's laughter
In innocence and wonderments
Swinging
Tiny legs pumping out in rhythm to the bluebird's tune
I love the feel of my lover's arms
Cradling me forever close…
The beatings of our hearts
One.
I love the sight of butterflies and bumblebees
Waltzing once again…
god's nectar safely
Adoringly
Cherishing

The inexplicable substance only they realize.
I love the tink, tink, tink of an early dawn's rain
Like notes played out
Brahm
Bach
Beethoven
A moonlight sonata
To follow
Soon after-the dried earth
Warmed
Dried
Still
The feel
The sound of gurgle, squish-squish between my toes…
I Love…

ICARUS' CLEW

For years I'd hopped and skipped
That labyrinthine journey
Icarus' Clew
Of silkworm strands
Fantastically mesmerizing
Intricately intertwined
Each dainty strand
Catching the inbetweenessinbetweeness
Colors—castoffs from yesteryears' rainbow
Stepping so slowly now
The dizzying memories
Of children's laughter
Now…fossiled
The path
A maze…
And I
Twisting
Turning
Flying
Flying
Icarus—
My muse
And through those
Nimbus
Clouds
Together
Leaving colorful clew strands
For some others
Not yet born.

DESIRE

Down one cobblestone street
Basket filled with long black roses
Night too quickly announcing
—claimed my youth
Standing in darkness
Silence .
Beneath the faded paper lantern
Wearing my scars
Time's jest…history
My womanhood-
Coming of age
Graceful
Fancying the feel of cashmere
Alpaca
D'ior
Shutting my eyes
As if
That might cease the screeching echoes
Of silence
Flores de muertes
Desire-

Mini Mort

I just awoke from slumber

That mini death seems to be shortening

As each new night blanket falls

Still

I cannot shake free (then again, perhaps, something...
someone-some time an antiquity hence-
ordained such awakenings and rehearsals)

That fear of NOT awakening

Paint me your magic night

Where dawns are ceaseless

And my tomorrows in soft whispers

Waltz to that Elysian

Peace.

Give rise

Again

My Id.

WE CALLED HIM
GOD FATHER

Dare you walk in his shadows
Your distorted visage
Of no consequence
Father has eaten through sinew and bone
The remainders
Beyond the righteous man
Whose proud fidelity meted out in
Honor and truth-
The familial
Living in that inner
Pantheon
Now, flocked by tourist
Seeking Knick Knacks
Adorning curios
Collecting dust—
I wonder if Agrippa minds?
Who've kissed the legacy
Birthed by the need
A resurgence of Robin Hood-
M-A-F-I-A
Esposito
Luciano Leggio(lightly)
Bosses coming
And going in a hail of bullets
And massacred corpses
Eyes agape
Silenced
Secrets
Bleeding crimson rivulets
In an unending journey down

One city street
To another
Give me alliance
It is
-Our thing-
Cosa Nostra
Family business
Family ties
Family…
Upon pain
Death
course for betrayal
A hangman's nooses
And five cent bullets
Marking the value of your betraying heart
And I shall remind you
One final time
Before infinity calls
Firmly grasp the face that…
Hid your truth…
God
Father…
One solid kiss upon each cheek-
And-
This I shall
I shall not forgive.

UNCIVIL I?

Redirection

Misdirection

Insurrection

Or?

Erection-

Oops-

Damn Freud!

In giant sweeps

Barefooted

Swiftly

Penned

A new

Wait…

The old order-

Garbed in a royal cloak

Embroidered with some new words

And old

Waving a gloved hand

An obscured

Distorted

Image.

Civilians

One by one

Well received

Masked

Editing their free speech

While untrammeled

Perhaps

Perhaps not—

And somewhere

Everywhere

Unfettered arms

Awaiting

Magical potions

And

Somewhere

Everywhere

Hunger pounds out

In unison

(it seems-do you not hear the woeful pangs waiting
for the rations of what curbside bins refilled, emptied,
refilled and yet, painful hunger grows)

Are you listening?

To the discordances

Deafening raucous

To the right

Left

And the blaring

Silence

Ear-piercing

In harsh unreality

Festooned

Do you not hear

Silence?

DEREREPROGRAM

Division
Revision
Belting the Battle Hymn
Manifest Destiny
Don't you know.
And I think
That i shall NEVER see a poem
As lovely as a tree
Reprogram
The impudent masses
Coloring outside the lines
Were you NOT paying attention
In kindergarten
Where everything the Curriculum outlined
Would be your forever truth?
Hey, Chagall?
Would you be so kind as to include me?
I mean. I. Want. To. Be. A. Violin. Playing. Goat.
Floating. In. A. Sky. Of. Ethereal. Surreal. Blue.
Life would be good
Then.
And by-the-way
Robert?
You were right all along
Ice does suffice…
When the world
DeReReProgram
Serves intolerance
Bigotry
Hate
And forgiveness
Kindness

Oops!
Pardon. Me. Not.
DeReReProgram.
Yadda. Yadda. Yadda.
Someone
show me how to color
Outside
The lines
Again.

ANCHORED

But for a second
The once frothy foam
Ceased its dance
With each weighted ship
Of carefree wanderers
Tossing down filled flutes
Of that 1990 Moet Chandon
Anchored down
Hunkered down
Painted faces
Peering hazels, blues, greens, browns…
To Rigil Kentaurus
Enviable Indignation
"The Nerve!"
Swatting Away
What
Only money can see-
Anchored-
Old money
New money…
Bourgeoisie…
Boorish-
Interlopers
On the fringe of…
THOSE not anchored
And floating
But. Not.
Upon the Dead
Sea-

EROSIONS 2

Perched upon a fragile branch
Loudly chirping
Emphatically announcing
In angst and discord
And it cannot cry-
And, OH! Such Resonance
Its wings
Muted
Matted
Frayed and Weather Worn
Recalling daybreaks
Soaring
Good Morning, Sun!
Juxtaposed
The budding of magical
Azure
And Purple Mountains
Majesties-
Deftly by that unseen…
Be friend? Foe?
Strutting with your
Formidable Talons
Pecking
In order
Until…
Reliable
Disdained
Disrobed
Wind
Erosions
And—
Just like that—

Purple Mountains
Majesties
Sand and the memory of
A Warbling's Final Chirp.

CLEO

I thought I caught Cleo crying
As she stood beautifully stoic
Strong
Watching
Decades hence
Will she still...
And when to the breech
Angry voices
In frustration
Mayhem
Mistrust
Betrayal
Found...
And echoes streaming against that calm
Perhaps
Perhaps
Per chance
Liberty's toll
Will not be
be so spirit crushing
-Cleo braces for...

Random Meanderings

Caught in a wet paper bag

Held between the then and now

While chaos with slumped shoulders

Heaving a burdensome satchel

Of uncertainties and fears

Bellows out in protest

Knowing the truth

But for those cursed rose colored glasses

Crushed in misguided protests

Amassed through historical

This and that...

And kingdoms for a horse

No one would ever ride

Far far in search of a Utopia

Where all unfolds

Displayed like

Bakery items

Aromas still sifting through the crevices
of bolted windows and doors…

But for that wet paper bag

Too long burdened

Undone

Reveals a world…

Where like fleas upon a dog

Have scampered in frenzied haste

Looking for what, why, and how

they may never find-

And resignation sets in

In hopeless abundance

As the puppeteers continue the pulling of invisible strings

And ennui sets in-

HAIKU

Upon kitten paws
Memories flit in and out
As night lifts her veil!

A SMALL WORLD

There was a time when the world was very small
And all I knew of it
Was from the tales my mamma told.
A time of lollipops and paddy cake
Of sleepy lullabies
And skipping stones upon the lake.
Hershey kisses, nana's homemade lemonade
Under the summer sun
And learning to give for giving's sake.
Playing hide 'n seek or tag—you're it
Chasing butterflies
And wearing mamma's shoes that never fit.
Donning cherry clusters upon my ears
A fairy princess was I
But, the world grew larger through the years.
Young women and young men
Marching Marching
To fight other's fights in a distant land.
No longer would I remember the tales my mamma told
Or play pretend
Fearing nothing…fighting dragons—I…so bold.
And as the world grew larger and larger I saw
In the Day after day
Newscasts of lives lost in the far far away war.
Then, one day and I'm not sure why
The world became smaller
And many would die.
A virus created by someone they say
Traveled the earth
Carrying Panic and Fear on that very same day.
Soon, I forgot those tales my mamma had told
Death wasn't real in the then

As sad reality's fangs quickly took hold.
Thousands dying-some not very old.
I learned about hate, injustice, and relearned left and right
While again the world grew smaller
And things seemed to change once again overnight.
People took to their homes and bolted their door
Hiding and waiting
For whom or the answer to when or the what for.
And all that was heard came from a box or a screen
Friendships distant-re-shapen
Wondering…lamenting the what could have been.
There was a time when the world was very small
And all I knew of it
Was from the tales that mamma told.

NIGHT FALLS

Where will night find you?

Dwelling for far too long

In the sad yesteryears

Or reliving those moments

You danced between raindrops

Or

With your wings

Feathered white

Lying in that pristine white blanket

Creating angels

Beneath the barren dogwood

The one

That just yesterday

The sun caught your laughter

As you swung

Your tiny legs pumping out

The seconds…

Thinking of the yesteryear

When dad scampered up-

(He was so much younger…

As I)

That dogwood

Lassoing That Branch

Shimming down

With calloused and often

Bleeding fingers

From yesteryears' toil

Pounding rods into

Those rails

Preparing journeys

Neither of you would take…

Oh! But for yesteryears

Daddy giving me a gentle push

My hands so young

Soft

Lassoing my daddy's rope

Perched upon that trailer tire...

Angels fly

Daddy in the yesteryears

-I thought I caught his smile as night fell

And the moon

Peering through those aberrant clouds

Just yesteryears...

Just yesteryears.

THE HIDDEN TRUTHS

In the distance
Painted faces
Blurred
Distorted
A well cherished Picasso
Eyes filtering in
Colors-
Damn be Rose-Colored Glasses
They are…
Blinded by manipulations
Machinations
And the-
Eliminations of those
Seeking a truth…
Disrobed
Redressed
So like the Emperor
Convinced he walked in royal gala…
And in the final moments
As final tithings were offered
By the ivy eating lambs
She offered no apologies
And as the final current
Announced the truth
No one listened
The blind did not see
Nor care to…
Leaving the earth
As she had come-
But for that knowledge that she knew what she had not known
Making
Taking mental notes

As the lights flickered
So much as those final
Shudders
…spent lovers
Reaching the apex
In the final throws
A whisper
To sleep-

MAMA WILL ALWAYS REMEMBER HANDPRINTS

· ·

Years from now
You may miss the then
Wonder
Perhaps
If you loved too much
Or not enough
Long after tiny handprints have faded
And that blanket
You know the one your mama gave you
Just as her mama had given her
And back
And back
And back.
Back when you slept some
Or not at all
And oh! So often just watching that incredible
Miracle
Sleep
Suckling fingers
(One just wouldn't do)
Dreaming, perhaps, of fairies in the grand azure
Running to catch the elusive unicorn-
With golden ringlets
Her crown
And mama her sentinel
Forever keeping watch
Even now in the distance-
And in the somewhere
Another...

ATTICUS SLAVE
AND MASTER

Slurring out his words
One letter at a time
Had he stood silent
A pregnant pause
Hiding just behind
That noble's stare
With shark teeth and powdered wig
At a time when no lives mattered
But...
Not one would speak ill
Of—
His deeds
Duplicity
Juxtaposed
Freedom
Imprisonment
And the valiant
His golden mane
Brandishing that virgin sword
Still...
Dull
Slashing through
The smell of metal
Dried blood
Blanketed by new
The distant drone
Of oars forever
Churning
An incident
Valor and dishonor
Sifting in plumes of grey
It's Tea Time!

MY DESERT BOOT

Heavily my foot lands upon the sands of the Sahara-
In its massiveness, it is the largest, after all,
I shall find my way.
I shall seek the oasis where Dromedary camels come to rest-
If only for a short while
Taking in water that will hold them over
Many days.
I shall drink... I shall drink
And in doing so, I shall come alive
Again.
It is real, that oasis, after all
And while my Desert Boot weighs heavily
Upon my foot-I'll ignore the discomfort it brings
And move on
Further into Africa searching out
The beautiful flat-footed Addax
And make my way along the sandy landscape of the Sahara's.
I shall not be easy prey for the poachers
Who may seek me out-
I shall outlast them all-
They will not feast on my me and...
Rip my leather.
I am stronger, more cunning than they
realize... I will not be easy prey.
My Desert Boot helping me along
Farther into the vast Sahara
Greeting the horned viper, whose horns protect its
Eyes
against the sand-
Camouflage
Though I do not expect it to be so
As I travel in the daylight-

my Desert Boot, pinching, weighing heavily-
I shall ignore the pain of it-
And farther into the great Sahara I shall go-
Still greeting, with my Desert Boot, a Dorcas gazelle. That has
found some leaves from trees and bushes. And watch it for a while-
I shall eat the fruit of the trees-
If it will share-
And take berries from the bushes
Should some be there.
The farther I traverse the vast, relentless miles
of sand, the heavier my Desert Boot
Like the noose that held me in check
As I made my way down the cement walks
Of bustling, chaotic, frantic streets
Squeezing myself into overcrowded subways
that took the ghost-like and worn faces
Of people, a mingling of smells, and the grinding Halt of squeaky
wheels here and there Marking, announcing exits, my exit.
There is no oasis in the city
No respite for me and my heavy Desert Boot.
So I travel and explore.
Watching, just watching a monitor lizard
Who so reminds me of cold-blooded souls
In that subway or frantically scampering to
I know not where
Nor do I care.
I so prefer to sit upon the sand and
Watch, just watch as the monitor lizard,
Out in the extreme heat of the great Sahara
And I am unafraid... I am unafraid
I do not wish to fight
And the basking lizard, like so many
On those chaotic city streets
Will look upon me pityingly as I sit,
my Desert Boot reminding me of pain, restrictions.
Frantic, hurried life along the treeless city pavement.

Yes, I shall sit.
Released from a self-imposed captivity of heart, body, and soul.
I too, like the lizard, sometimes chooses, shall flee.
And my Desert Boot, I come to realize
Will continue to pinch, cramp, and remind me-
I so prefer to travel, most times, alone
Wrapped in my own thoughts
Thoughts that would not come so easily
Good thoughts
Thoughts that enabled, encouraged me to find
My oasis-
Where I may drink to satisfy my soul
Then, and only then, shall I know
Contentment and renew my need to create
Express my thoughts using vibrant colors
That reveal my those thoughts, my soul
In agony and joy
And I shall overcome the reminders my Desert Boot offers.
And if I choose to bury my head in the sand, like the
Ostrich perhaps along the busy city streets,
And those...
Who do not welcome the possibility of reaching
Their oasis-
Greeting others, welcoming their habits, their needs
You see, they do not own my Desert Boot!

WHERE ANGELS FLY

In the distance

Where angels fly

Above music of that forever

Where all life

Echoes out in resonance

A will free

And smile despite the obscured

Starlight

Suspended just above the overgrowth

Cha Chas and Mambos

The sensual flow

One step

Two

My feet in rhythm to that tune

A Mother's night

Watching angels fly

Watching angels fly!

MAMMA'S PLAYGROUND

Mamma cuddled her nursing babes
In her heaven's gilt
Rocking back and forth
Back and forth
Her voice dancing in the distance
Where cubs
Upon that ancient tree
The one witness to the birth of the artist's pallet
Time in increments
Playing beyond
The mortal's ground
And joyful cubs
Scampering up
Down
Up
Mamma's gentle fingers
Still soft upon their fur
A game of peek-a-boo
And a celesta-
Resonates
Ethereal
Bells
From the distance echo
And mamma's cubs
Holding on!

BIRTHDAYS AND REMEMBRANCES

I am that wave

the crest

The surface

In joyful moments of life's tenderness and
happy sprinkles of my youthful essence

I float effortlessly

My eyes wide

My spirit soars

Hitching the occasional ride

Upon my unicorn's back

And in less joyful moments

When wayward demons

Would have me drowning in that ocean's trough

I welcome the respites

Between sorrow and ruminations

Find me upon that vertical distance-

Between crest and trough

Gliding in seemingly effortless butterfly strokes

Against the undertow

today

today

I am time

Marked by the ebb and flow of escapades

Charades

And the seconds of helplessness

Hopelessness

But for that ebb and flow…

I dare with impudent determination

Cast away that which would greedily

Swallow my last breath…

Not today

Not today…

ON GOLDEN PATHS

And in the end
A gathering commenced
Light the touch of one hand
Many more to follow
Guiding the lost
Helpless
Hopeless
Confused
Seeking out the Golden Paths
Where the pipe organ played
Out in tune to the steady March
Pulsating
Resonating
In the happy memories
Yet
Fragmented
Hues of Hallelujahs
Hitching a slow trudge
To that place where all compositions
Begin
Light the touch of one hand
In the distance of the nebulous
Uncertainty
Beyond the land where angels gather
And unicorns pranced upon cotton clouds
Nymphs
Trolls
Fairies
And
The illusion of that Leprechaun's pot
A fading sheen
Fool

The only reminder
Within the admired
Patina of that millennia pot
The Leprechaun
With his taunting snicker
But for mere mortals
Caught.
One hand
One hand
Solitarily meandering above
The echoes of Hallelujah
Where the flickering lights
Mourn the passing
Reminders
That forever regret
The contentment and—
Self
Reaching out with that wooden batea
Sifting out
The dust
covering the tired earth
Too long counting out the passing
Of one hand
One hand
On Golden Paths
Where a blaring crescendo
Floats
Falls
Upon that final Hallelujah.

ANGEL TEARS

Deep beneath

Before

Beyond

Over and-

Above

Angel tears

After…

That…

With a deafening gulp of grief-

Wearily dabbing at opaque crystals

Too quickly dried

Where once her alabaster skin

Feared not the rising of that solstice sun

Maximum declination…

With avarice and greed

Ate away the remains

Hidden in the underbrush...

Pity comes too late-

Fated...destined...

What words will soften the fall-

What words-

Shall ease your mind-

I'm here-

Take my hand-

Rise and in majestic rhythm to your soul's song

Rise-

Rise!

ANGEL TEARS 2

Test my patience
As your face
Contorted
Your sharp fangs
Hitting upon that once loving
Me
Who in infant naïveté
Trusted
It was so much simpler to believe
Love
Honor
Cherish
Till death
Oh!
Had I realized through those peeks through
a romantic's fanciful artifice
Beyond the blooming flora
Of varying fruition
I might have heard
A troll's chortle
Sifting through the
Blah
Blah
Blah
And yaddayadda
Of monotonous recitations
As that amateur harpist twanged and plucked
On that taut string
So wishing an escape-
Test my fortitude
Strength
Resilience
I shall rise.
I shall rise!

NOT LONG AFTER

Wearing mamma's fuzzy pink slippers
Shuffling two-year old feet
Along that worn plank floor
In just above a whisper
Like the ocean's foam caressing pink sands
Of the Ethereal-
Her tongue formed patterns
Only few would hear
And mamma watched from yesterday
When daddy's laughter
Like a surprise summer storm
That
Brought the dry Earth to life
Filled the knotholes where critters gathered
Brown her ringlets
Her crown
A sachet back
And two…sometimes-more
Forth
With nothing but a hand-me-down
Crotchet purse
Where she safely hid her dreams-
And mamma
Still in yesterday
Watching.

OH! CHILD OF MINE

Where were your tiny legs
Steadfast against your rocking horse
In rhythm
Against
The pelting rain
Just outside the window
Pane
Taking you?
Oh! Child of Mine!
What journeys had you taken
Sitting tall
In that wheelbarrow
Grandpa kept
Just outside that weathered barn?
Oh! Child of Mine!
How many pebbles skipped
Upon the water
Happily in the sounds
Of the Splish Splash
Before that deep bed welcomed them
Home?
Oh! Child of Mine!
How did yesteryear become forever?
In chaos and anguish
And
Oh! Child of Mine?
Riding upon your paddle board
Fighting the angry sea
With its furious foam
Slapping-
Beating in raucousness
And dissonance…

Ear-piercing-
Where?
Oh! Child of Mine!
Had your escape-
Your body sedate
Your soul in haste
Sprinting to meet up with
The after?
Oh! Child of Mine!

IN CURRENTS

Where will you be when early dawn
Unfolds and kisses
The horizon?
And I
Curled up
Bunched up
Wishing you…
Wishing you…
Before that longing
Stills
That sultry
Whispering and…
Honey-lemon tea kisses
Taking the last of my ecstasy
To the rise in
Passionate
Spasms
Meet me
'Fore
Daylight
Breaks
You and I…
Where
Will
You
Be?

TIME'S ILLUSION

Had I not skipped that beckoning path
Barefooted in my youth
Spying white winged butterflies
Waltzing beneath a joyous sun
Plucking petals along the way
The yes and…
The no
A Sing-song
Bouncing off the aureate silvers
Of last evening's mist
Now guiding my steps
To a magical castle
Just beyond that cursed effluxion of
Time
Had Time's Illusion
In reverend hope of discovering
The new
The ancient
The now
What if?
In fanciful
Fickle
Youth
Without my kaleidoscopic mind
Truth was as innocent
And
Unbeguiling
As my unvarnished soul…
The Yes and No…
In Time
Illusion
In eager anticipation

And vexatious echoes
Reality-
Mortal
As I may be-
Time!

BEFORE THE LAST

I imagine you swimming against the current
Desperate to catch your breath
As that rip current
With its octopus tentacles
Tangled you
Captive-
Grim snickering in that immeasurable distance
And I
Silent-
The steady
Deafening sound of hissing
From that man made support
Pumping out in cacophonous music
Like a toddler
Banging out tunes of his newest drum set-
And a gurgling
Silence
In an ear piercing dread
As my mind catches
The forever touch
Of your hand
Folded in a baby's warmth
Walking to the park
Where you watched...
From your favorite bench
This girl pumping her legs
Upon that weathered swing
And that summer breeze catching
Our breaths-
They came so easily then-
Before the Last-
And in that...
Weep out
Words I'd wish I'd said.

ODE TO THE LIZARD KING

Careening down the Champs-Élysées

The cacophonous echoes of those souls in chaos

Living at that place

Ignoring my Purple Heart

And that sweet taste

Of honey lemon.

Had I-

Would I-

In those colorful, compartments

Like life reminders and...

Around my neck?

Beads...

A collection of dreams lost-

Found-

Amidst the rankings of the bourgeois

On a journey of futility

I escape

And in purple dreams

Walks the Lizard King!

LEFT UNREAD

How could I not find
The answer
To that question that filled the air
When all was still?
How could I not have seen that behind
That carefree smile
Nothing was real...free?
I imagine as the sky-
Nebulous-
you peering through a heavenly curtain-
Strumming out tunes
On your guitar
That lifts the stars to-
Pirouette-
Battement...
In an end...repose?
I had not felt the icy
Reach of that...now...
Too familiar reaper-
In vermilion-wine
The taste of metallic...
Spitefully lingering in the air-
My lips...
You mouthed out your answer...
With a serene disquiet...
And I
Black lace and a hangman's noose-
Tighter...tighter
My question
Caught between nooks...
And smiles-

Hockey pucks-
Rock Star posters
And books left unread...
Answer.

WHEN PRUDENCE ESCAPES

Oats upon the water
Slowly in surrender
And defiance
Succumbs
And beneath the miasma
Of empty glass
Coke
Bottles
And rusted tin cans
The mouth agape
Like in that
Final
Scream
Breathe again-

THE LOST DARE
NOT DREAM

Yet…
Here we are
Lost
Strumming the taut
Strings
Of our air guitars
And dance in rhythm to the solitude
Of daybreak…
Were we to sleep
Our music would be lost
For those who have no dreams.

THE LOST DARE NOT DREAM 2

And in those moments as early dawn
In dewdrop rhythm
Dance upon the eager
Folds
Of my window garden
Where lavender…
Impatiently
Sways to a celestial rhythm from that angel's lute
My body running among the Neverland
Where mere mortals dare not visit
And in that sweet repose
My mind does yield
To that distant song…my angel's lullaby
To dream

SUNDAY

Cover my ecstasy
With your lips
As I fall deeply
Into your eyes
A final
Fall of a dwindling
Star
In a sweep of-
Before
During
Now
Nectar
Oh!
do bring
Me
Gently
Exhausted
Fulfilled
With
Twilight
Kisses
Upon my throat
Gutteral
Whimpers
Crying
Out
Love

Autumn Calls

Sloth Summer Days
Retreating
Caramel
Apple
Crisps
Pie
Fritters
Pumpkin
Spice
Cozy
Campfire
Nights
Wrapped
Toasty
Warm
Watching
Amber
Sparks
Dancing
In your eyes...

WHEN TERROR CALLS

Where will you go when Terror calls?
Will you slither beneath the Sea
Hoping each ebb and flow washes it away?
Will you be covering your eyes
Wishing it away?
Will morning find you...
Naked and afraid-
Your soul ripped apart in the dead of night?
Will you hide your face and muffle those
Deafening wails only you can hear?
Will you
When Terror calls
Gulp your words
While your knuckles
White beneath that olive skin
Grip at that pungent smell
That will forever hang in your air?
Will you
Find that magical fountain
Of innocence rediscovered?
Will you build that impenetrable wall
With its restricted entrances
To your thoughts
Experiences
Terrors...that guarded facade
Burdened by that past
Which hasn't truly passed
Just yet?
When Terror Calls-
When Terror Calls...

MY ANGEL MUSE

Call you
My Angel Muse
Strumming out my mind's dissonance
While my lonely alabaster canvas
Wails
Grieving
Strum out upon your lyre
That cursed vanity
Bring you your gatherings
Of the long ago
So tenderly clustered in my satchel
Awaiting…
Call you
My Angel Muse
Bring your silver
Your red limestone
And sun-kissed remembrances
Of possibilities
Where artifice
Lays exposed
Disembodied
Call you
My Angel Muse
Tomorrow comes too late.

FUZZY BROWN BEAR SLIPPERS

I left your fuzzy brown bear slippers

Beneath your bed

So longing to watch your toddler feet

Safely snuggled in that well-worn synthetic fur

Scamper about

Your imaginary friend by your side

Your hand high in the air

One thumb up

Swatting Away fire-breathing dragons

And only creatures you could see

Gone…

But for the fuzzy brown bear slippers

And the frame-

Reminding me of your tiny hands…

Forever in place upon your waiting empty room-

Hands forever tiny

Caught in child safe paints…

The mom's day surprise

Brought home from 'The Little Lambs' nursery school

And that memory…

Though others sift through

Now…and AGAIN-

As your eyes caught mine

With a hint of shadowed images of the dragons

You had not slain…

And the forever of your mirrored smile

As you stepped out

One final time…

To the breech

Thumbs up…

THUMBS UP

Words jumbled

My brain pelted

By the resounding

Ping

Ping

Ping

And from somewhere

Somewhere

A voice

At times in soothing syllables

Like those my mom

Would comfort me to sleep with...then

Later

Now

The sound of voices in discord

Like the broken strings of my guitar

The music?

Gone...

Had I not needed

Wanted those

Now and again

Reminders of my ivory pick

Caressing each...strand

Those conflicted

Voices playing

Fist-a-cuffs with my psyche

Maybe would have had no-

effect upon my being

none at all-

Voices-

In incongruity

Maniacally

Taunting my waking thoughts

Weighing my body down

My soul too willingly

Follows…

And that cheeky grin-

Masqueraded…

My thumb at attention

It's all good-

Thumbs up-

I'm okay…

I'm okay…

And in that moment

The not before

The not the after

To stop my pain

Those unrelenting echoes…

Rose higher

Than I…

And in the still

When birthdays come and go

And the this or that

Those things we collect

On the anniversary-

The birth-

The Christmas past or

Yet to come...

Thumbs up

Thumbs up

To them all...

And in the after

In attendance

Those voices in unison

A sing-a-long

To the days

For the days

When you watched

You knew

What I so wanted

To never let go

For you

For you-

Thumbs up!

TIGHTER!

In his arms

Where the chaos of the world seeps in haphazard rivulets

Gathering

The forgotten

Maimed

Homeless

The helpless

Hopeless

Resting their cracked tumbles of...

Hair held in place from the discarded

Cracked

Flimsy rubber

Once protecting hordes of vegetables

The ones that ancient

Stoic vendor still peddles

On street corners-

But now

in his arms-

Love

His comforting love

Brings me to tears

And were I one to will my eyes

-close

In reality

My senses...

Huddled closer...

To feel...

To make his breath-

his existence my own...

Hold me-

Tighter

Tighter

TIGHTER!

Weave a fantastic tale

Where fear is slain

And carried off into-

Oblivion…

And entombed

Do NOT mark

That end…

Just remind me of why we LOVE-TIGHTER

TIGHTER

TIGHTER!!

WHERE HAVE THE DAYS GONE?

• •

Where have the days of bath in the kitchen sink?
And raspberry tummy kisses-
Boo-boo bunnies chillin'
Just in case-
Your little fingers playing run and chase
Baby peas-
The ones that always wound up on the kitchen floor-
And peek-a-boo-
Though you knew just where I'd be
Would always be-
Watching
Waiting
Hoping
That you'd always stretch those open
Toddler
Arms
Up and over that crib rail...
The one you'd often use as a teething toy-
Crying
Laughing
And often-
I'd watching
And catch you smiling at angels
As you cuddled
My arms...
Never wanted to let you-
Go...
Where are the days of snowman bubbles in the sink...
Or tottering on your baby scalp...
Of squeezing rubber ducks-

That hooded towel
The one I saved for days…
Just like these…
Where have the days of kitchen sink baths gone?

WHEN THE REAPER CRIES

Soldiers at attention
In monument stances
One by one
Shoulder to shoulder
Faceless aberrations
In stoic attention
Clawed feet planted
Upon the frigid length of
Vostok Station
With hollow stares
Chained waiting
Here...
And-
Along the treacherous paths of Annapurna
K2
Waiting a call to...
Attention.
Wrapped
In cocoon blankets
Of heavy iron links-
Boulder anklets
And maggot carved out hearts
Leeches-blood engorged
But, always wanting more.

Awakening Shadows I

It was not long
Trudging down that isolated
Social Path
With its ashen scores of psychopaths
Blank
lying
To themselves
With great conviction-
And in nightmares
Walk…
Scooping up others along the way…

Awakening Shadows II

Where my heart leads
My mind may follow...
The sun's reflection
Casting bursts upon that ancient
Dial...
Time...
Time and the turning...
Spring-
Summer-
And in the mask of autumn ambers...
A social path-
A melting of thoughts-
As Father Frost-
Thaws out that dormant psychopath-
He's been so cold for so long
In the shadow of mind...

STIRRINGS

In a disquieting ache
Consummated
Eating away the what if's
What might have beens
While that frigid gust
In bursts of desires
Longings…
And an unfathomable regret
Heavily…
Crushing
Those memories
Of those infants' coos…
Angel wings' kisses
And sleepy smiles
Upon those cherub faces
Long they'd waited
Cradling…
The barren womb
Once…
That once…
Before the furious wind…
Pelted at the hems of their skirts
Exposing alabaster skin…
And life's cavern of discord…
Where none would seek-out
Again-
But for that furious Southern Wind
That bore…a note
Upon which an angel's sweet breath…
In hues of baby blue-
Did reach those moms' musings…
The what if's

What could have
Been-
Do you remember me?
I remember YOU…

THIS CHANGELING'S GIRL

In innocent days of Knick Knacks and Paddywacks
This wayward girl
Collected worms-
Feeling their hearts beat
Between her dainty fingers
As they slithered and squirmed
In benign protest-
Catch-
Release-
This wayward girl
With chestnut gazes
Listening to her inner song
Brown ringlets...mother's halo
For this wayward girl
With muddied hands
Clench
Unclench
A squish...gurgle
Before the sun...
fall
This wayward girl-
The Changeling's Girl...
Night terrors
And that palpable dread
Suspended upon her bedroom wall
White fanged-
Eternity
And Hell
Thus...
Wails this wayward girl...
In screeches
But for that White-Fanged Eternity
Only she can hear.

PAINT ME YOUR WORDS

A Moment Ago
And
A Second Ago
In varying shades of blues-
Golds
And a...
Hunter's Green
In joyful delirium
Life called with a gentle nudge
And a kitten's purr...
And it was then-
Just... A Moment Ago
The Source and I
Were...
Reunited-
And in that Second Ago
I captured an illusionist's
Hidden truth-
Upon that noble artist's
Canvas...
A Moment Ago...
A Second Ago-

CRYSTALLINE TEARS

In tranquility
Solitarily
In the frigid early dawn
Her majesty drops her crystalline
Tears...
Each alighting effortlessly
Upon My Gentile
Earth
Awaiting its rebirth
When she will...
Reach up
With old familiarity
Caress
And lovingly kiss
Each of her majesty's
Teardrops
Away...
Collecting some-
With the remains...
Of a dove's discarded feathers...
Whispering...
In her voice
Adagio...
Piano
Piano...
Only her majesty can hear...
Awakening
Awakening...
And in those moments
In those moments
Crystalline
Tears
Earth's memory
And Rebirth-

In Depression
and Divinity

• •

Between the joy and turmoil
Falls the rain
In moody…somber
Hues of a sadness
Churning…
Gathering fragments of thunderbolts
That haphazardly stomp…
At times…releasing-
That inexplicable ennui-
Depression-
But for those times
When that intangible
Cursed-
Weighed down-energy…
trickles and frothy dew…
Screeches out
Divinity…
And were i to rise-
In plumes of demonic thoughts…
Discover…
That spirit
Spitting out…
Venomous loathing
And I
Drawing in those
Darker hues…
And explore the farthest
Lightings
Somewhere

Above
El Greco…
From the view-
Above Toledo!

MY ASTRAL LIFE

And while I lie slumbering

Beneath a Blue Moon

My body

Still

A respite

My mind traversing

Lifting

And it was there

Just…then

My soul

In rhythm to the quivering

Golds

Of the night's minuets

That I recovered

From…so long agos

THERE IS…JUST NOW?

and all was quiet
along the city streets-
and the occasional stirrings
of the night
just behind the filled garbage bins
echoed
up
then down
concrete fortresses
with their makeshift placards…
Closed-see you soon-
and
there
though no one dared to rustle back their
white lace curtains-
windows closed against…death
a sound
disquieting-
fearful-
with anticipation
of tomorrow lasting
longer than
any before
or after-
travels
from house to…
house-
carrying aberrant hope-
there exists a helplessness
while catching glimpses
of dug out trenches
stacked-four-five high…

the unclaimed-
perhaps…
but
loved just the same…
and my mind overwhelmed
my eyelids heavy
from lack of sleep…
words
come and go-
BUT
mostly come
AND stay-
and Spring trees
Tulips
and Daffodils
are not as pretty as last year
or the year before that-
and
Yes-
I fear
they may never be again.

LOVE ME NOW

Tears like shards of glass

Crimson

droplets

Cutting

scarring

Slowly

crusting over

Where flesh

meets flesh

Slowly

a shattered heart

follows

Forgive

me

even when…

that old-

clock

ceases vigil-

and time is but-

A Passing

of what?

and tears no longer scar-

EXORCIZING THE MONSTER

-And on that day
White became my enemy-
In spatters, drops shouted out-
A Jackson Pollock masterpiece
Convergence
Divergence
All misaligned
When all colors faded
-And on that day
I was…
The woman who became faceless
Nameless
An actor upon-
Stage 4
-And on that day
My body an aberration
Inhabited by that Monster
Avarice-
Unforgiving-
-And on that day
The exorcist arrived…
Radiation
Chemotherapy
Lumpectomy?
Mastectomy?
-And on that day
I played the actor
Stage 4
Desperately clinging
To the very last-
When I could learn to love
…Jackson Pollock once again!

My Mother's Road

Steps solidly planted

The road scattered with the remainders of washed out prints-

I have walked

Run

Skipped

Hopped

And on occasion

Danced

Hot upon my back

The sun

Sifting the early dawn's remains

Of nebulous clouds

Slower

So much slower my pace

The road shorter

Harder to attack

Horizon's song

Filters out and up

Scooping up the falling stars

And I

In awe

Wonder

If I may find them

One day

One day

One day-

And in my well-worn shoes

I shall

For the now

Continue on-

THE LITTLE GIRL SURVIVOR

In fantastic journeys of page after page
When thoughts of lost innocence
Betrayals
Broken promises
&
Chaos
Crashed & burned
In my brain-
I traveled
Through a mirror
Down a rabbit hole
Gunga Din
Brought me life
Scout-my friend
Atticus
Ridding society
Of rabid
Creatures
I was safe!

TIME'S WARRIORS

Youth hastily retreats
Leaving
Time's Warriors
With life
In varied hues of splendor
Etched upon their faces-
Stronger those who
Have taken chances
Made mistakes
Wisdom their trophy
Touching
Hearing
Experience's beckoning
Indelible remnants of …
Mortal beings
Brandishing
Kindness
Love
Compassion
Oh!
Do not fear night's allure-
Humanity
Your legacy.

A BED OF LIES

I found that frayed flannel
You loved-
Your smell lingered
Embedded
Nestled
In the fibers-
And in that moment-
You flooded my mind
A lingering
longing
For your touch
Fingers combing back stray strands
Caught
Clinging
Covering my eyes
After the loving
Set it on the stoop
Outside
In the winter's frost
Waiting
With memories.

My Purple Satchel

Oh, innocent child
Always skipping
Stones
Watching their dance
Upon Waters
Your purple satchel of Dreams
Beaten by unforgiving time
Still your most prized
Treasure
And-
You manage to scoop
Up possibilities
Your heart
Racing
Imagining
The what if she-
Could skip
Upon the water-

ESCAPING

Hold me closer
When night falls
And those relics
Haunting
Fears
Of abandonment
Weave caustically
In need
obnoxious
Greed
Box cutter
Teeth
My heart
Mangled
Toxic
Metallic
Wisps
Marking
An imaginary
Boundary
Of where
Holding
Wanting
Loving
Escaping-

SUNSET AWAITS

-there
Just
beyond
light
Is caught
Upon the fickle clouds
I stand
Barefoot
toes anchored
Curled
Clutching
An ancient stone
Shadows of the past
Just
That-
in the final set
that golden sun-
I greet
Evening's blanket
My innocent
Infant soul
Quieted-
Calm

Upon the Comforting Sea

. . . .

...and upon the tranquil sea
My vessel–
Alights
Nestling
Dearly
Lovingly
My loving memories
My only cargo
Drifting north
Where my happy soul
Joins the ethereal
Horizon
Cascading
Gentle
Remnants
Of amber
Sunsets
Along the way

My Bipolar MOM!

She danced like no one was watching-
I was!
Curled up on the couch
Fetal
Crying
Like no one cared
I did!
My mom passed-
And in those final moments-
She mouthed-
Help me!
Holding her hand-
Brushing back the lose strands
Of gray hair
Her face
Once porcelain
Natural pink blush
Now muted
Pale
She danced
Danced
Danced…

HOLD ME

-with your smile
Seek my soul
Your eyes
Gathering it up
Soothing away reminders
Love lost
Carve out a niche
In your heart
Making mine
Beat in rhythm with yours
Hold it there
For I so want to be held
And as dawn awakens
Our slumbering
Let it find us
Making love

AN ODE

...and as that final paw print
A memory...
Seeped slowly-
Into the joining...
Of my hardwood floor-
Where it would remain
Undisturbed-
Collecting specks of dander
Vacuum
Never caught
I snuggled
Deep
Wrapped my pain
In his favorite blanket-
Breathing
Out
In
Triggering
Memories-

Hiding
My happy
Smile
Porcelain
Face
Revealing
Nothing
Camouflaged
Flawless skin
Pursed lips
Dare not speak

Blank eyes
Waiting for the Shadow
Fading
Greeting
The sunless
Sky
Behind that
Painted smile
You know Me-
A face greeting
Faces
Along my way-
(Tapio Haaja)

Life as a Metaphor

I am a dragon
Fear me not
My flame has long since been-
GONE…
I am poison ivy
Clinging for life
To that dying
Willow
That WEEPS
NO-MORE
I am an hourglass
White sand
Dampened by the dew
Grey
Clings to cracked
GLASS
And
I AM
TIME-
I AM

RISE AFTER THE FALL

F
A
L
L
With great uncertainty
What awaits my landing
Into that cloaked night
Where so many
Gone before
Never to return
Wondering
As I remember them…
Who will remember me?
E
S
I
R

TIME

Time
Reminders
Measured in nanoseconds
Etched
Memories
Of youth
Beauty
Lost-
Oh! Sweet vanity-
Mind not the aging
Flesh
Forever
In the
Tic
Tic
Tic
My soul
Holds
Beauty
In endless
Passions
Reposing
And
Time…
My universe.

LAURELS

Early dawn found
Me
Outstretched
Arms
Hungrily
Feeding
Off first daylight
Laurel wreath
My crown
Wishing
The impossible
Possible
Unicorn fancies
Strumming a guitar
& fairies
Dancing
In the heavens
Gulping
Down the last of the setting
Sun
My unicorn takes
Flight
&
Summer
Ends

...AND THERE ARE DAYS

...and there are days when the world implodes
And I am funneled violently into its abyss
It matters little
And I mind it not at all!
It is in this miasma of bits and pieces of things
As I had so wished them to be...
That I find the chaos of it all too familiar...
And words chewed well and spat out
Collected by my already weighted mind.
...and there are days
When a lonely, tattered, and beaten soul
Is found with nothing left to give...
So scoop me up in formidable talons
Rip my heart, consume my everything
...and there are those days
When laughter is annoying
Love conditional
And the more you want, the more I give
Alas, there is nothing left
But for a solitary stump
Waiting to provide a respite
...and there are days
When hugs are not comforting
Kisses sandpaper rough
And loneliness fills the void
No body, no heart, no soul
Just an abscess that was once the impetus
That gave rise to hopes, dreams
The could have, should have, might have
Created, and often did,
My mind, me
Coloring each open space with possibilities...
And then there were days!

REDBUD

Feeling
your warm breath
Caressing
My neck
As cotton candy clouds
Settle beneath
A summer sun
it
Peeks
Through
Lavender
Twisted
Weeping
Redbud
Playing fist-a-cuffs
With
A summer
Breeze
Impatient
Sighs
retreating
2 lovers
Now
1
warm
Breaths
My lips
redbud

SHADOWS

Sinking
Forever
Deep
Into your eyes
Darkness
Fading
I acquiesce
To what
May
Come
Innocent
Kisses
Under the blue
Moon
Just
You
And
I
Making
Love
Tender
Slowly
Catching
Falling
Stars
Our bodies
Shadows
Beneath
The jealous
Light.

REMINDERS

Lavender
Juniper
Jasmine
Daffodil
Awakenings
Pulling
Me
Reminders
Of not
So long
Ago
A little
Girl
Chasing
Butterflies
Caught
Under
Their
Melody
A slow
Dance
Eyes
Shut
Breathing
Time
fluttering
wings
Unfurling
Majesty
Caressing
Blossoms
And I
Just
Dance!

ENCORE!

Birthing
My soul
Escapes
Alighting
In flawless
Wisps
Forever to be
Etched
Then scattered
In golden
Hues
This muse
This beautiful muse
My fancy
My dreams
Impassioned
Spirit
Forever
After
A few words
In scansion
Sonnets
Rhythmic
My pen and paper
A ballet
Pli'e
Chass'e
Encore!

-AND PASSIONS FUSE

Melting in your arms
butter
Under the desert sun
Smooth
Smoky
Sounds
Played
On a saxophone
Rhythm
Deeper into the jungle
Echo
Thunderstorms
10thousand years
Now
Bodies
Sweat
Fire
Searching
Coveting
Ecstasy
taaffeite
Lying here
Your taste
My golden street!

HUES OF AMBER

A tired old barn
Holding
memories
Sacred
Ladder
Hayloft haven
Watching
Amber sunsets
Tossing
Turning
Upon emerald grass
The distant
Whistle
Clickety
Clack
Coal fueled
Train
Spewing
White
Gray
Plumes
Clickety
Clack
As the aging
Crows
Balter
From the leaking roof!

DEFENSELESS AND...

Do play
Your golden sax
My body quivers
And I so want
More
Sensual
Erotic
Oh
Too
Tease me
Fill me
With your
Rise
And
Runs
Unnerving
My senses
I'm ready
Voodoo
Spell
Happily
I succumb.

SET THE ALARM

There are gargoyles afoot
Some rolling in on evening tides
Razor talons sifting pink sand as they go—
Some swooping down in packs
-in darkness
Feasting on chaos and causticity.
Some from beneath the shifting plates
with magma orbs
But
All living upon the stench of hate.
Gratified
they trample (some with horny toes) the remnants
of a cornucopia…of malcontents…rich…poor…young…old…
yeah…those
too.
Chuckling (as Gargoyles do) at the Rip Van Winkles
who stretch, yawn, and roll over—
Sleeping till the alarm, they never set, wakes them.

IN FALSEHOODS
AND FALLACIES

Somewhere in the not so long ago
Voices strong
In momentum-
Purpose-
Each syllable distinct
Chimed out
…and those skeptics
Cried foul
Their rationale
(borne…perhaps…from ignorance…—
And pardon me, your bigotry in falsehoods and fallacies
thrives and momentum, with a slight of hand,
crashes down catching-throwing-fostering
dispersions-such realities
belie the seen—)
But, voices strong
Echoing
Break the silence
to improve it all
don't you know—
turn away from the garish
game of pretend
Where the valiant-called to arms
Another Punic War
(One of many yet to come)
and have you gathered your bits of this and that
just in case
just in case
the meek really should inherit
Mother Earth

and, as I am…too
One woeful sigh
the last
before the sun sets
In Falsehoods and Fallacies.

PUPPET MASTER

Too long silence followed my wayward steps
Listening to a woodpecker
Pecking in cacophonous rhythm
The barren limb of a once majestic
Ancient
Llangernyw Yew
Felled by the ravenous blizzard
The very same one
That covered city sins
As toddlers-noses pressed against shoddy window
Panes-
Dreamed of snow angels
And daddy's coming home…
Dressed in those comforter (though they weren't very comforting)
Venturing out…anchored in red made-for-toddler sleighs…
Lost in the whiteout of it all-
We didn't mind the constant burst of prestige crystalline treasures
(Our eyes tightly sealed while, in eager anticipation—
our mittened hands-grandma's last Christmas offering-
outstretched-such the Puppet Master…)
From that place where (some believe) orchestrates such majesty-
Down one hill…daddy steering
As I struggled, with mittened hands-simultaneously
catching snowflakes and crystals upon my eager tongue
Daddy's frayed cloaked—warmth my salvation!

THE VORTEX

Beyond those tumbles
My arms outstretched
The spirited sun
In mischievous barbs
Passing mockingly above the throbbing
ache…my mind-
Adorning my head-
The Medieval Maiden
In golden hues of mocking possibilities
Probabilities…
The truth-
Swatting away my youthful…naivete
Fickle fantasies of golden headdresses-
Passing over
Under
My neck-
Extending-
In Arms and-
Armor
Nobly I dance
upon the barbed wire-
…in the Vortex
where I always welcomed the parade of jesters
—my innocence—
Aching for… Angel lutestrings
And laurel crowns
fashioned by that spirited sun
The Vortex…and I
unhooked-
Possibilities…extending far-
Beyond-
Above-
Freedom
-and my childhood naivete.

She will NOT yield

· ·

Sitting back
Mamma catches her breath
though those whimsical winds test her strength
Yielding is never an option
Her aria dulce
piano
forte
humming along
Testing that warrior always-
always in fierce defiance through tempests fierce
She will NOT yield!!

THE HOARDER OF DREAMS

Here he goes again…
And again-
The Hoarder of Dreams-
Double-tongued…slurping a few
While those razor talons
(Having trampled each flicker under a moonless sky)
Shred the remainders…
He's not Mephistopheles…
I wonder-nonetheless.

WHEN I DIE

When I die, I will not lament the golden road outstretched to its
Own will
I will not pine the hunger for unsatisfied passion.
I will not hold in judgment those seeking only my survival when
I yearned and sought to live instead.
I will not stand unwelcoming at the foot of the altar
All those before me who know not where I loved.
I will not yearn another second in the existence of that translucent
Solitude.
Alone I will not go forth-back and up
Again.
I will not question the moment that will follow
All those that came before-
weeds beneath the open meadows-
I will not hollow out my heart
Replace it with cotton clouds of doubt
This I will know
That I will know
And in the knowing will be my existence
Still.

MY OPEN WINDOW

Infinity strumming upon your borrowed harp
Each note gingerly bouncing off the sleepy clouds
And as night unfurls its glorious coverlet
In mystical fancy…
Lovingly
A tender peck upon each
Stars float in-
My Open Window-

PAUL SIMEONE

Paul Simeone is a pianist/vocalist/composer who has been making music since he was a child. From his days playing the accordion at age six to his current role as a solo and group performer, he's always held the gift of music in a prominent place of his life. Before recently retiring, he was the choral director for 35 years at Ridgefield Park Junior/Senior High School in New Jersey. He's performed in numerous venues over the years, playing various styles of music (pop, R&B, Broadway, jazz, etc) and is still performing live today. He has recently started working with Anna Arrigo on providing music for her poetry, namely "Ain't Got No Time" from "Changeling" and "Closer" for "Anima" ("Closer" can currently be found on SoundCloud). Of all the aspects of making music, he has experienced throughout his life, composing and recording his own compositions is still his favorite activity. Paul and his wife Lori are currently spending their semi-retirement years living happily ever after in New Jersey…

More of Paul Simeone's music is available on SoundCloud, Spotify, Apple Music, Amazon Music Unlimited, YouTube Music, Pandora Radio, iHeart Radio, Tidal and Deezer.

ANNA CASAMENTO ARRIGO

Anna Casamento Arrigo was born in Sorrentini, Sicily, and came to America with her family to settle in New Jersey many years ago.

Tragedy struck when she suffered a life-altering stroke. Conventional therapy helped, but writing proved to be the greatest therapy of all when she turned to creating poetry to express her inner-most thoughts and fears and desires. Music also provided inspiration, and after combining aspects of music, prose, and classical literature, she devised her own style of writing, something intensely personal, almost visionary.

Prior to her stroke, Mrs. Casamento Arrigo taught many inner-city students, inspiring them to do better. Children need inspiration, and once they find it in themselves, they are capable of anything. That is her motto, and she has used to pass on her knowledge to her five children and her twelve grandchildren. For her, learning is not enough. Imparting that knowledge to others unselfishly remains her focus in life.

She has penned numerous books in a variety of genres including her memoir, a romance novel, several collections of poetry, this is her seventh, as well as several children's books. She does not want to be tied to any particular genre and wishes to explore the limits of each genre she chooses to write in.

In terms of her personal recovery, Mrs. Casamento Arrigo continues to strive to regain what has been lost. Writing provides that spark of creativity, one that she has used to create more children's books as well as a series of short stories plus another memoir. Currently, she is working on creating one more collection of poetry that showcases her love of life and all that we can be.